KITTY

BLAM!

NICK BRUEL

BAD KITTY

Does NOT Like
THANKSGIVING

ROARING BROOK PRESS

New York

Kitty does not like Thanksgiving.

Kitty **LOVES** Thanksgiving.

Kitty loves Thanksgiving for one reason—

TURKEY!

Kitty does not like green beans.

Kitty does not like mashed potatoes.

Kitty does not like cranberry sauce.

But Kitty **LOVES** turkey.
And today is **THANKSGIVING!**

Kitty likes to call this day
**"YUMMY-YUMMY-
ALL-OF-THE-TURKEY-IS-MINE-
AND-GOES-IN-MY-BELLY-
DAY."**

Kitty, leave the turkey alone!
You have to share on Thanksgiving!

Kitty does not want to share.
She wants the turkey
all for herself.

Kitty decides to TAKE
the turkey.

Kitty has a plan.

There go the green beans.

There go the mashed potatoes.

Kitty has
another plan.

NO, KITTY!

There goes the cranberry sauce.

Kitty, leave the turkey alone!

You ruined the green beans.
You ruined the mashed potatoes.
You ruined the cranberry sauce.

BAD KITTY!

NOW YOU CAN'T HAVE ANY TURKEY!

Poor Kitty.

Kitty does not like turkey anymore.

Kitty does **not** like Thanksgiving.